Rachel Isadora
I SEE

Greenwillow Books, New York

Library of Congress Cataloging in Publication Data
Isadora, Rachel.
I see.
Summary: A baby responds to all
of the things she sees.
[1. Babies—Fiction.
2. Visual perception—Fiction]
I. Title.
PZ7.I763Ias 1985   [E]   84-6104
ISBN 0-688-04059-4
ISBN 0-688-04060-8 (lib. bdg.)

E
ISA
7/86

For Gillian Heather

I SEE MY BEAR.
GOOD MORNING.

I SEE MY SPOON.
I EAT.

I SEE
MY BELLY BUTTON.
TICKLE, TICKLE.

I SEE MY STROLLER.
IT'S TIME FOR A WALK.

I SEE THE SLIDE.
WHEE.

I SEE THE CAT.
MEOW.

I SEE MY BALL.
I THROW.

I SEE A BIRD.
FLY AWAY.

I SEE MY BLOCKS.
ALL FALL DOWN.

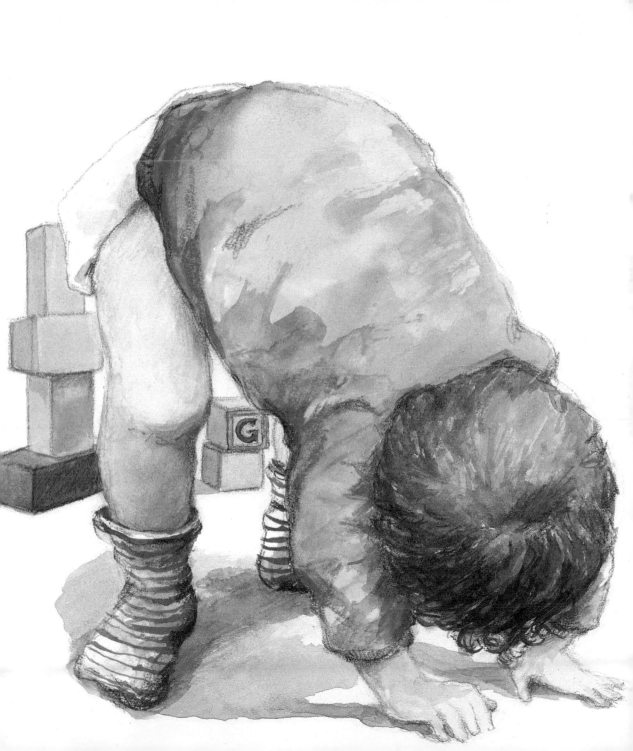

I SEE MYSELF.
HELLO.

I SEE MY BATH.
SPLASH, SPLASH.

I SEE
MY BOOK.
I READ.

I SEE
MY BOTTLE.
I DRINK.

I SEE MY CRIB.

GOOD NIGHT.